The New Adventures of
MARY-KATE & ASHLEY™

The Case Of The
Mall Mystery

Look for more great books in

The New Adventures of
MARY-KATE & ASHLEY™

series:

The New Adventures of
MARY-KATE & ASHLEY™

The Case Of The
Mall Mystery

by Alice Leonhardt

HarperEntertainment
An Imprint of HarperCollins*Publishers*

A PARACHUTE PRESS BOOK

PARACHUTE PRESS

Parachute Publishing, L.L.C.
156 Fifth Avenue
New York, NY 10010

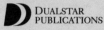
DUALSTAR PUBLICATIONS

Dualstar Publications
c/o Thorne and Company
A Professional Law Corporation
1801 Century Park East
Los Angeles, CA 90067

▄HarperEntertainment

An Imprint of HarperCollins*Publishers*
10 East 53rd Street, New York, NY 10022

10 9 8 7 6 5 4 3 2 1

CHOCOLATES GALORE

"**P**atty, what are you doing in there?" I knocked on the pink door of the ladies' room stall.

"I *told* you," our friend, Patty O'Leary, yelled from inside. "I'm changing into my costume!"

My twin sister, Ashley, checked her watch. "It's been thirteen minutes and twenty seconds," she reported. Ashley likes to be exact about things.

"If you don't hurry up," I called to Patty,

"you're going to be late for rehearsal!"

Patty was performing in an International Talent Show at the mall tomorrow. Since Patty's mom was out of town on business, Ashley and I thought Patty might need someone to cheer for her after she practiced her dance. So we grabbed our friend Tim Park and asked Mom to take us all to the mall after school.

When we got to the mall, Mom decided to do some shopping. But Tim was stuck waiting for us outside the bathroom!

"Hey, Patty!" I tapped on the door again. "Come on out. If Tim has to wait for us any longer, he might explode."

SLAM! The door to the stall flew open.

"Ta-da!" Patty stood before us wearing an emerald-green velvet dress. She was smiling from ear to ear.

"Whoa!" Ashley gasped. "That is one cool costume!"

"See?" Patty flipped her long, curly red

hair over her shoulders. "I told you it was worth waiting for."

I stared at Patty. Her costume was beautiful! The skirt was big and full. It had three pleats in it that were lined with shiny silver satin. Silver shamrocks and harps had been stitched into the top of the dress.

Patty held a matching green cape lined with the same silver satin.

"Patty, you look like a princess," I told her.

"I should!" She sniffed. "My mom had this costume made especially for me."

I shot a glance at Ashley. She shook her head a little. I knew exactly what she was thinking. Patty's parents got her anything she wanted. Sometimes she acted a little spoiled.

"Come on." Ashley pushed open the bathroom door. "Let's get going."

The three of us walked into the mall. I glanced around for Tim. At first, I didn't see him anywhere.

"Uh-oh. Where is Tim?" Ashley asked,

her blue eyes scanning the crowd.

I snapped my fingers. "I bet he's visiting Jimmy at Chocolates Galore!"

Chocolates Galore was one of the many carts set up around the talent show stage. It was famous for dipping just about anything—fruit, marshmallows, lollipops, even potato chips—into chocolate! Tim's older brother Jimmy worked there.

"Well, let's go get him." Patty sighed.

My stomach gave a growl. "Right, and while we're there, let's buy some chocolate-covered pretzels. They're my favorite!"

We walked past the stage where Patty would be practicing. It was decorated with colorful flags from many different countries. The area around the stage was crowded with parents and their kids who were performing in the show.

Five carts stood in a half circle in front of the stage. I read the names on each of them—Go Team Trading Cards, Make Up

Your Mind Cosmetics, Totally T-Shirts, Chocolates Galore, and Sparkle Jewelry.

"Hey! Over here!" Tim waved at us as we approached the Chocolates Galore cart. "I thought you guys would never come out of that bathroom."

"Hi, Jimmy," I greeted Tim's older brother.

"Hi, guys," Jimmy called to us. He dipped a strawberry into a vat of warm chocolate. "Want a sample?"

"They're delicious!" Tim smiled, showing us his chocolate-covered teeth.

Ashley and I each took a strawberry. We thanked Jimmy and bit into them. The chocolate melted on my tongue.

"Yummy," Ashley said.

"I'm glad you're enjoying my chocolate," a man called as he strolled up to the cart.

"This is my boss, Mr. Voler," Jimmy told all of us.

Mr. Voler had on brown pants and a brown jacket.

"I like your suit," Ashley told him. "It makes you look like *you* have been dipped in chocolate."

"That would be very bad for me." Mr. Voler laughed. "I'm allergic to cocoa, which is an ingredient in chocolate. I would never stop sneezing."

"And he has the loudest sneezes," Jimmy added. "They're like volcanoes erupting. Ah-ah-ah-choo!"

"What can I get you ladies?" Mr. Voler asked. He winked at us. "I always try to wait on the pretty girls myself."

Ashley smiled. "We'd like a box of chocolate pretzels. If it won't make you sneeze too much," she said.

"I'm fine as long as I wear these gloves." Mr. Voler pulled on a pair of plastic gloves. "If I didn't have them, I would get very sick." He handed Ashley a box of pretzels.

"Anything else?" Mr. Voler asked.

"Nothing for me," Patty answered. "I

have to keep my costume perfect. And that means no chocolate anywhere near it."

"You must be one of the talent show contestants," Mr. Voler said.

"Uh-huh," Patty answered. She reached into her cape—and pulled out a sparkling green-and-white pin.

"Wow! What is that?" Tim asked.

"It's my mother's shamrock pin," Patty told him. "It has real diamonds and emeralds in it. And it's good luck to wear it."

I stared at the pin. It sparkled so much, it almost hurt my eyes to look at it.

"It's really beautiful." Mr. Voler leaned toward Patty for a closer look. Then he turned to Jimmy. "Why don't you go on your break now?"

"Cool!" Jimmy gave us a wave and took off.

Ashley touched Patty's pin with one finger. "I can't believe your mother let you wear it."

"Yeah, uh… just help me fasten my cape with it, okay?" Patty handed Ashley the pin. Ashley carefully slipped the pin through two loops in the front of the cape and closed it.

"Now, that's perfect!" Patty cried. "With my lucky shamrock pin, I'm guaranteed to win the talent show. Let's go. Practice is about to start!"

Patty led the way over to the stage. Then she stopped walking so fast that I bumped into her. And then Ashley bumped into me. And Tim bumped into Ashley.

"Ow! What's the holdup?" Tim complained.

Patty pointed to the stage. "No way! That is totally unfair!"

THE STOLEN SHAMROCK

I turned to see what Patty was pointing at. It was a girl, waiting for her turn to rehearse. I recognized the girl from school. "That's Dee-Dee McGee. She's in third grade." I stood on tiptoe and waved to her. "Hey, Dee-Dee!"

Dee-Dee came over to us. She was carrying two plastic pots planted with real shamrocks. "Hi," she said. "Are you dancing a jig, too?" she asked Patty.

"No, I'm doing a reel. That's harder."

Patty stared at the shamrocks. "What are you doing with those?"

"Using them to decorate the stage for my dance," Dee-Dee explained.

"That's not fair!" Patty whined. "I didn't know we could decorate the stage."

Dee-Dee nodded. "Sure. I put palm trees on the stage last year when I did my winning hula dance." She gazed at Patty's sparkling pin. "Hey, that is really cool."

"Thanks. It's my good luck charm. It's made of real diamonds and emeralds," Patty pointed out.

"Wow." Dee-Dee reached toward the pin.

"Don't touch it!" Patty pulled away. Her elbow hit one of the pots. It crashed to the floor, spilling shamrocks and wet dirt everywhere.

"Oh, no! My shamrocks!" Dee-Dee cried.

"Oops," Patty muttered. The four of us started to help Dee-Dee with the mess.

"Don't worry, I've got it," Dee-Dee told

us. She scooped two handfuls of mud off the floor and plopped them back in the pot. Then she carefully replaced the shamrocks.

"I'm going to go give these some water." Dee-Dee set off toward the water fountain.

Patty checked her watch. "I get to practice on the stage for only half an hour. I need to start now!"

Patty started to fan herself. "Is it hot in here?" she asked. She took off her cape and laid it on the stage.

It wasn't hot at all. I think Patty was just nervous.

"Will you guys do me a favor?" Patty asked. She dug out a tape from her backpack. "Give this to Sonny Davis. He's the master of ceremonies. We call him the emcee."

Patty pointed to a man standing near a microphone at the front of the stage. He had blond spiky hair. He wore a white shirt with a black vest and black pants. "Tell that guy to start the music right after I put my hands on my waist. Like this."

"Sure," Ashley answered. She took the tape from Patty. "We'll bring it over right—"

A humongous sneeze drowned out the rest of Ashley's words.

"Mr. Voler," Patty, Tim, and I said at the same time.

I laughed. "Maybe *he* should be in the show. Those are amazingly huge sneezes."

Patty shook her head. "Not amazing enough to beat my dancing feet." She started doing some steps of her Irish reel.

Dee-Dee came back from the water fountain with her pot of shamrocks. She set the pot on the ground and watched Patty. She frowned as Patty's feet moved faster and faster.

Ashley started to clap. Tim and I joined in. *Screeeeeeeeee.*

A piercing screech rang from the speakers. I clapped my hands over my ears and squeezed my eyes shut.

The screeching seemed to go on forever. When the sound finally quit, I took my hands off my ears. I opened my eyes and spotted Sonny and his crew gathered around the microphone.

"Wow. I hope they fix the sound system before the show," Ashley said to me.

"Nooooo!"

I jerked my head toward the sound of the shriek. It was coming from Patty.

"What's wrong?" Ashley gasped.

Patty cradled her cape in her arms. "Mary-Kate! Ashley!" she cried, a look of horror on her face. "It's gone! My good luck shamrock pin is gone!"

3

A CLUE ON THE CAPE

"**M**y pin! It vanished. Disappeared," Patty wailed. "My mom is going to be so mad. She doesn't know I have it!"

"What?" Ashley exclaimed.

Tears filled Patty's eyes. "I sort of took the pin from her jewelry box without telling her—or my dad."

"Yikes," Tim muttered.

I stared at Patty. "That is *not* good."

Ashley gave Patty's shoulder a squeeze. "Don't worry. We're detectives, remember?"

"That's right." I jumped in. "Olsen and Olsen are on the case."

"Maybe it fell off and bounced somewhere. Help me look!" Ashley called. Tim, Ashley, and I began to search the floor in front of the stage.

"Maybe it rolled under the table where the judges will be sitting." Patty pointed to a table at the side of the stage.

I crawled under the table on my hands and knees. But I didn't see the pin anywhere. "Sorry, Patty. Nothing there," I announced as I headed back over to her.

"I don't see it either," Tim added.

"That makes three of us," Ashley said, standing up.

Patty sniffled. "We have to find it before my mom gets home."

"How could it just disappear?" Tim asked.

I gulped. "Maybe it didn't disappear. Maybe somebody—"

"—stole it," Ashley and I finished together. We do that sometimes. It's a twin thing.

Patty's eyebrows shot up. "*Stole it!* How? We were standing right next to the cape."

"Right, but when the speaker made that terrible noise, I shut my eyes," I said.

Ashley nodded. "Me, too."

"Me, three." Patty bit one of her fingernails.

Tim's face turned red. "Me, four."

Ashley took out her pen and pad from her fanny pack. "Mary-Kate, we need to talk to everyone who was near the stage. Maybe one of them saw who stole the pin."

"I think we should tell Sonny Davis, the emcee, what happened, too," Patty said. "He's in charge. He should alert the mall police."

"Great idea, Patty!" I exclaimed. "Plus he had a perfect view of us from the stage. Maybe he saw something important."

I scrambled onto the stage. Ashley

climbed up right behind me. We rushed over to the emcee. "Mr. Davis, someone took our friend Patty's shamrock pin," I explained. "It was on her cape, but now it's gone. She's very worried about it."

Sonny turned toward us. "What? A missing pin? How terrible!"

"It's made with real emeralds and diamonds," Ashley added.

"This needs to be reported to the mall police," Sonny said. He made a note on his clipboard. "When did she notice it was missing?"

"Just now," Ashley told him. "We were standing right over there when the pin disappeared. Did you happen to see anything suspicious?"

Sonny ran his hands through his hair, making it even more spiky. "I was concentrating on getting the sound system set up. I didn't notice anything. But I'll make a report as soon as I get one free second."

He turned to one of his crew. "Try it!" he yelled.

A blast of Spanish music rang from the speakers. At the sound, a boy in a sombrero leaped onto the stage. He let out a loud whoop. Then he threw down his hat and danced around it.

"Wait, wait! Hold on a second!" Sonny called to the boy. "This is just a test. You'll get a chance to practice later."

"Mr. Davis! Mr. Davis!" Patty climbed up on the stage. "I get to practice before the Mexican hat dance, right?"

Sonny checked his clipboard. "Right, right. You're doing the Irish reel."

Sonny took a crumpled wax-paper sack out of his pocket and pulled out a chocolate-covered cookie. He popped it in his mouth. "You can start your practice now. Where's your tape?" he mumbled as he chewed.

"I have it." Ashley handed it to him.

"Mary-Kate, do you mind getting my cape?" Patty asked. "I need to retie the laces on my ghillies." She knelt down and started undoing the ties on her dancing shoes. They looked kind of like ballet slippers.

"Sure." I hurried over to the front of the stage, where Ashley had placed Patty's cape. I picked up the cape and gasped.

"Ashley," I called to my sister. "Come over here quickly! I found a clue!"

EATING THE EVIDENCE

Ashley climbed off the stage and hurried over to me. "A clue! Where?" Patty and Tim ran over, too.

I held up the cape and pointed to brown streaks on the satin lining. "Look! Muddy fingerprints."

"From Dee-Dee McGee!" Patty cried. "She had mud on her hands from her spilled shamrocks. Plus, she was near the cape when the pin disappeared."

I glanced around, trying to find Dee-Dee.

She was all the way over on the other side of the stage—and her hands were still dirty.

I turned to Ashley. "I think Patty's right. We have our thief."

"Let's go get the pin back!" Tim cried. He started toward Dee-Dee.

Ashley grabbed him by the elbow. "Not so fast. We don't have enough evidence yet."

"What are you talking about?" Patty demanded. "She knew my emerald-and-diamond shamrock was a lot better than her plain old plants. She knew that with my lucky pin I'd beat her."

"She did look upset when she was watching Patty dance," I added.

"We still need proof," Ashley told us. "And I know how to get it. All we have to do is get a sample of the mud on Dee-Dee's hands. Then we can compare the color of that to the mud on Patty's cape."

"If the colors match, the case is closed!" I grinned.

"But how are we supposed to get some of the mud off Dee-Dee's hands?" Tim asked. "We can't just go up and ask her."

"The pretzels!" I burst out.

"Huh?" Patty crinkled up her forehead.

I gave her a sneaky smile. "Trust me. I have a plan."

While Patty started practicing, Ashley led us around the stage to Dee-Dee. We passed a boy in a cowboy outfit practicing a lasso trick. We wove around two girls doing the hula. We squeezed by a boy dressed like the Tower of Pisa.

Finally, we reached Dee-Dee. She was standing to the side of the stage, in front of a pet store. We stopped a few feet away from her. I opened the box of chocolate pretzels. "Anybody want one?" I asked.

Tim dove in with both hands. I think he'd eat rocks if they were covered in chocolate.

"Anybody *else* want one?" Ashley asked. "Dee-Dee, how about you? They're really good."

Dee-Dee stepped up to us. "Thanks." She reached for a pretzel, then froze. "Oops. My hands." She held them up so we could see the mud streaked on her fingers.

"Here. Wipe them on this." I handed Dee-Dee a tissue. She scrubbed all the mud off her hands. I made sure to take the tissue back from her the second she was through with it.

"Um, we should go watch Patty now. We're her cheering section," Ashley said.

"Sure. See you guys later. And thanks for the pretzel," Dee-Dee called after us.

We ran back to the cape. Ashley spread it out over the judges' table so the mud streaks were easy to see. I held the dirty tissue up next to it.

"They look like they're about the same color," Ashley said.

Tim leaned closer. He turned his head from the tissue to the cloak, then back to the tissue. "Same color," he agreed. "But not the same smell."

"What?" I asked.

"If there's one thing I know, it's chocolate," Tim bragged. He pointed to the streaks on the cloak. "And that is definitely chocolate." He sniffed deeply. "I looove this smell."

I nudged Tim away and stuck my nose in the cape. "Tim's right. That is a *chocolate* fingerprint."

"It's still a good clue, right?" Tim asked.

"A very good clue," Ashley told him. "But it also eliminates Dee-Dee as a suspect."

"That's true," I agreed. "So we have to look for people who were near the cape with chocolate on their fingers. There can't be many people like that around here."

"I don't know about that," Ashley said. "Look over there." She pointed to three kids eating chocolate-covered graham crackers. "And over there." She pointed to a man eating a chocolate-covered banana on a stick.

"And over there." Tim pointed to a woman in a flowered hat. "She's eating chocolate-covered fudge. Man, I'm getting hungry again!"

I glanced around the mall. Everywhere I looked I saw someone eating chocolate from Mr. Voler's cart. I let out a groan. "Nearly everyone in this whole mall is a suspect!"

5

MICE ON THE LOOSE!

Ashley sat down at the judges' table and pulled out her notebook. She wrote down: "Clue #1: Suspect left chocolate finger-prints."

I thought hard. "Well, we know one person who has been eating chocolate *and* who was close to the cape when the pin was stolen," I said. I jerked my head toward the stage. Mr. Davis was walking away.

Ashley nodded and made an entry in the notebook that said, "Suspect #1: Sonny Davis."

Ashley tapped her pen against the note-book. "But Sonny told us he was going to report the theft of the pin to mall security. Why would he do that if he is the one who stole it?"

"Hmmm." I pressed a finger to my lips. "If he reported the theft, then it would seem as if he wanted the thief caught. That would make him seem less suspicious to mall security."

Ashley nodded. "Right. Let's keep him at the top of our list and—"

Ashley's words were drowned out by a loud "ah-ah-chooo!"

"Mr. Voler." Ashley, Tim, and I giggled together.

"Maybe he should sell something besides chocolate, since he's so allergic," Ashley commented.

"Maybe," I agreed. "Hey! We should talk to Mr. Voler. We could ask who he sold chocolate to in the last—"

"Eeyaaaahhh!" The loudest scream I ever heard echoed through the mall. Before I could even try to figure out what was happening, another screamer joined with the first one. Then a third scream.

"What's happening?" Ashley yelled.

"I don't know," I shouted back. I whipped my head from side to side. Someone needed help. More than one someone. But who? And where?

Ashley grabbed my arm. She held it so tight, I could feel each of her fingernails. "Mary-Kate, look down."

"Oh, no!" I cried.

A stampede of furry white mice was heading straight for us! Their noses twitched. Their rubbery tails swept back and forth. Their little claws clicked across the mall floor.

"Legs up!" Ashley ordered.

I jerked my legs up onto my seat at the judges' table. Ashley yanked her legs up, too. Tim leaped up onto the table.

I tried to count the mice. But they were moving too fast.

"Don't panic!" a tall man in a white coat called out. He was running after the mice with a big wire cage under one arm.

"The mice are from my pet shop. They're pets! Harmless pets! Please don't panic!" he begged. "And please, please, please don't step on them!"

The man bent down and scooped up a mouse. He gently placed it in the cage.

"We'd better help," Ashley said.

I stood on tiptoe so I wouldn't crush any of the mice. And so none of them would run over my feet.

"Got you!" I heard Ashley cry. I looked over and saw her putting a mouse into her fanny pack.

"My turn," I said. I reached down and grabbed the closest mouse. It squirmed so much, I almost dropped it.

"Oh, no, you don't," I told it. "You'll get squished if you go back on the floor." I pulled up the bottom of my T-shirt to make a little basket and dropped the mouse in. Then I dove for another one. I didn't stop diving for mice until my T-shirt basket was full.

"Bring them to me," the man from the pet store called. I raced over to him. He helped me transfer all my mice into the cage.

Tim ran up a second later. He had a load of rescued mice in his T-shirt, too.

"Thank you so much!" the man from the pet store said. "I have no idea how the cage got opened." I noticed he wore a name tag that read "Pete."

Ashley hurried over. She began unloading all the mice in her fanny pack.

"I think we got all of them," Tim said.

I glanced around. "I think you're right," I answered. I noticed a large bulge under

Pete's white coat. "Do you need help getting those mice into the cage?" I asked. I pointed to the bulge.

"No! Don't touch it!" Pete burst out. "I mean, no thank you," he said. He turned around and ran back to his store.

"Hey, look," Ashley called. "Over there." She pointed to three uniformed security guards striding toward the center of the mall. A tall lady and a short lady ran to meet the guards.

"Something's going on. And I don't think it's runaway mice. Let's check it out." I hurried toward the ladies and the security guards. Ashley and Tim followed right behind me.

"The necklace I just bought from the Sparkle Jewelry cart was stolen," we heard the tall woman say to the guards.

"My bracelet was taken, too!" the short woman chimed in. "I had it in a Sparkle Jewelry bag. We were in the pet store when the mice got loose, and then the bag was gone!"

Ashley leaned close to me and whispered in my ear, "Mary-Kate. That's *three* thefts in one day. Do you realize what this means?"

"Yes." I nodded excitedly. "We have a real jewelry thief on our hands. This could be our biggest case ever!"

A Slippery Surprise

Ashley nibbled on the end of her pen. "Do you think we should put the mice in our notes?" she asked.

"Good question," I answered as I watched Patty rehearse onstage. "Maybe we should."

"Wait a minute. Do you two think the *mice* stole the jewelry?" Tim asked. He gave a loud laugh.

"Of course not," Ashley answered. "But the mice could be *connected* to the crime. I bet those ladies were too busy screaming at the mice to notice the thief."

"So maybe the thief let the mice out." I snapped my fingers. "Ashley, we have another suspect."

"Who?" Ashley asked.

"Did you notice how weird Pete acted when I asked if he wanted help with the mice under his coat?" I said.

"Yeah," Tim said. "He practically ran away."

"Hmmm. That is suspicious," Ashley admitted. "And it would be very easy for someone who works in a pet store to let mice out of their cages."

"Time to visit the pet shop," I announced. "We have to find out what that bulge under Pete's coat was."

We took off. When we reached the pet store, Ashley pressed a button on her watch. "That took us only sixteen seconds. Which means that when Patty's pin was stolen, Pete could have run over from the pet store while the mike was squealing."

I led the way into the store. "Hey! Puppies!" I said, rushing over to the glass cage nearest the door. "Ashley, look. They're a litter of little Clues!"

Clue is our basset hound and our silent partner. She helps us out on a lot of cases. We'd probably have this case solved already—if we were allowed to bring her into the mall.

"They're adorable." Ashley lowered her voice to a whisper. "But we're here to investigate Pete's bulging coat."

I forced myself to leave the puppies and spy on Pete. He was kneeling by the cage of mice in the back of the store. And he was snacking on chocolate-covered peanuts!

"He's looking pretty guilty," I whispered to Ashley. "He's got chocolate all over his fingers."

"And check it out—the bulge is still

under his coat," Ashley answered softly.

"Let's go talk to him," I suggested.

Ashley and I hurried over to Pete. "Hi!" Ashley said. "I wanted to buy a squeaky toy for my dog. Could you get that green one for me?" She pointed to the dog toy on the highest shelf.

"Wow. Ashley's good," I whispered to Tim.

"I don't get it. Why does she want a dog toy?" he asked.

"She doesn't," I answered. "She wants Pete to reach for the top shelf. Because when he does, his coat will slide up—"

"—and we can check out that bulge," Tim finished. "Great idea."

I nodded. Then I locked my eyes on Pete. He was going for the dog toy. Reaching higher and higher.

His coat slipped up, up, up. If it moved another inch, part of the bulge would be uncovered.

"Here you go," Pete said. He grabbed the squeaky toy and handed it to Ashley. His coat fell back in place.

Rats! I thought. *I'd better try something else. I have to get a look under that coat!*

I marched over to Pete. "Gee, the buttons on your coat are excellent. They're so…round," I said.

That was all I could think of to say. The buttons were ordinary white plastic.

"Uh, thanks," Pete said.

I leaned closer. There was a tiny gap between two of the buttons. If I could get close enough, maybe I'd be able to see exactly what Pete was hiding.

My breath caught in my chest. I saw a flash of green through the gap. Green just like Patty's pin.

"Do you know where these buttons came from?" I asked Pete. I leaned even closer.

And the bulge started to *wiggle*.

This was definitely not Patty's pin. But what was it?

The bulge under Pete's coat wiggled faster. I could feel my eyes grow wider. "What—" I began.

Then a pointy green head popped out from between Pete's coat buttons. It was a snake! It opened its mouth and hissed angrily.

"Yowww!" Ashley and I yelled.

7

A SPARKLING SUSPECT

The snake's tongue darted in the air. I leaped backward. Ashley gave a little squeak of surprise.

"What's going on?" Ashley exclaimed. "Why are you hiding that snake under your coat?"

"This is Susie," Pete said in a low voice. He glanced nervously at the other customers. "Please don't say anything. Some people are afraid of snakes. I don't want to scare the customers away."

"We like snakes," I told him. "But not under our shirts."

"Susie is harmless," Pete explained as he stroked her head. "She's usually in her cage. But somehow she got out at the same time the mice did. She escaped from the store. I had to catch her before anyone else saw her. You know how some people are about snakes. I was afraid someone might hurt her."

"So you stuck her in your coat?" Ashley asked.

He nodded. "Yes. All the yelling scared Susie. So I left her in there. The warmth helps her calm down."

Ashley and I glanced at each other. Pete wasn't hiding the jewelry, but we solved the mystery of the bulging coat.

"Did you see how Susie and the mice got out?" Ashley asked.

Pete shook his head. "Too busy. I had one customer who wanted to see one of the basset hound puppies and another one who wanted to know what the best kind of parrot food is. I was trying to help them both. Then I realized that Susie's cage and the mouse cage were open."

"Can we look at the cages?" I asked.

"Sure," Pete answered. "Susie's is the one closest to the row of aquariums. And you know where the mice are."

"Excuse me, but do you have Smelly-Sweetie dog shampoo?" a dark-haired woman asked.

"Oh, yes! Right this way." Pete headed toward the front of the store to help the customer.

Ashley and I walked over to Susie's cage. Tim joined us. Ashley leaned close to examine the door. "The lock looks fine," Ashley said. She opened and closed it a couple of times. "Susie didn't get out of this cage accidentally."

Then she held up her fingers. There

were brown smudges on them. "Chocolate," she reported.

"It could have come from Pete," I said.

"Or it could have come from our thief," Ashley answered.

"So—do we take Pete off our list of suspects?" I asked.

Ashley sighed. "I guess so. I doubt he would have had time to find Susie *and* grab the jewelry before he started rounding up the mice."

"And he seemed so worried about Susie," I said. "I don't think he would put her in danger on purpose."

"So now what?" Tim asked.

Ashley glanced at her notebook. "Let's check in with Sonny Davis. He's the best suspect we have."

"Wait—let's talk to the person working at the Sparkle Jewelry cart," I suggested. "Two of the stolen pieces of jewelry came from there. Maybe we can learn about our thief by finding out what kind of jewelry he or she likes."

"Couldn't we talk to Mr. Voler instead?" Tim asked eagerly. "His cart is right next to Sparkle Jewelry's. He might give us samples. And we know the thief loves chocolate."

"You're going to explode if you eat any more chocolate," I told him as we walked out of the pet store.

"But what a way to go!" Tim answered. He gave his stomach a rub.

Ashley and I were still giggling at Tim when we reached the Sparkle Jewelry cart. We waved to Mr. Voler a few feet away at Chocolates Galore. Then we turned to the Sparkle Jewelry clerk. She was arranging necklaces on a holder. She looked about Jimmy's age, and she had blond streaks in her hair.

"Hi there," the clerk said with a smile. "I'm Jennifer. How can I help you today?"

She moved toward us. I heard a clinking,

tinkling sound with every step she took. That's because Jennifer was wearing a ton of jewelry!

She had several earrings in each ear. And lots of bracelets around her wrists. *And* tons of necklaces, a half-dozen rings, and layers of ankle bracelets.

"Hi. We're trying to help a friend get back a pin that was stolen from her today," I said. "We think the person who took it stole some jewelry that two women bought at your cart."

"I couldn't believe that happened!" Jennifer exclaimed. "I felt so bad for them. You should have seen the necklace one of those women bought."

Jennifer gave a dreamy smile. "It was heart shaped. It had a ruby in the middle of the heart. It was so sweet."

She let out a long sigh. "The bracelet the other woman bought was adorable, too," Jennifer continued. "It was a rope of silver seashells. It would have gone perfectly with the bathing suit I just bought."

"Have you noticed anyone hanging around the cart a lot lately?" Ashley asked. She opened her pad, ready to take notes.

Jennifer shrugged. "There are always lots of people around." She pulled a paper bag out from under the counter. "Chocolate-covered jelly bean, anyone?" she asked.

"Me!" Tim said. Jennifer dumped a bunch in his hand and popped a couple into her mouth.

Ashley stared at me. I knew we were thinking the same thing—Jennifer was a chocolate eater! Was she another suspect?

"Did you see anything at all during the robbery?" I asked. "The women were in the pet store when it happened." *You were definitely close enough to run over to them and take their bags*, I added to myself.

"Sorry, I was too busy dodging mice," Jennifer said. She gave a shiver. "I hate them. They give me the creeps."

"Well, thanks for your help," Ashley said.

We walked away from the cart. When we were out of earshot, I stopped. "Did you see all the jewelry she was wearing?"

Ashley nodded. "She looked like she could have been the display."

"Jennifer *loves* jewelry," I continued. "Do you think she took the necklace and bracelet for herself? She would have known what was in those Sparkle Jewelry bags."

"She was eating chocolate, too," Ashley added. "And her cart is near the stage. She could have taken Patty's pin."

I nodded, getting excited. "And she knows all about jewelry. I bet she'd know that the shamrock had real diamonds and emeralds in it."

Ashley turned to the page in her notepad labeled "Suspects" and wrote "Jennifer, the Sparkle Jewelry clerk."

8

UNDERCOVER

"**W**ait a minute. Jennifer can't be a suspect. She's afraid of mice," Tim reminded us. "And you think the thief let the mice out."

"Good point," Ashley said. "But maybe Jennifer loves jewelry even more than she's afraid of mice."

"Hey, guys." Tim's brother, Jimmy, came up to us. "How is the talent show rehearsal going?"

I shot a guilty look at the stage. Patty was still practicing. *It's more important to find her pin than to clap for her*, I decided.

"Don't you ever work?" Tim asked his brother.

"Mr. Voler likes to give me a lot of breaks," Jimmy answered.

"Ahhhhchooooo!" A thunderous sneeze rang through the mall.

"Speaking of Mr. Voler," Ashley joked.

I glanced over at the Chocolates Galore cart. Mr. Voler dabbed at his nose. Then he returned to dipping pecans and laying them on wax paper. "He needs to get a new job."

"Let's go talk to him about who has been buying chocolate today," Ashley said.

"What do you want to know that for?" Jimmy asked.

Before I could answer, there was a huge crash from the direction of the stage. I spun around. The heavy red stage curtain had fallen!

"Get me out of here now!" someone hollered.

Ashley gasped. "That's Patty yelling!"

"We've got to help her," I said.

Ashley, Tim, and I ran over to the stage. When we got there, Sonny, the stage crew, and a female security guard were already lifting the heavy curtain. Patty crawled out from underneath it.

"Are you okay?" Ashley asked.

"Yeah," Patty answered. She smoothed her velvet skirt. "My costume didn't get ripped or anything, did it?"

"I'm Officer Benson," the security guard announced. "Who can tell me what just happened?"

"I checked the ropes that hold up the curtain myself," Sonny said. "I don't understand why it fell."

I moved closer to the curtain and studied the rope. My heart started thudding in my chest. "Ashley! Come look!" My sister hurried over to my side.

"Chocolate!" I pointed to the chocolate

fingerprints that were up and down the rope.

Ashley's lips were pressed into a straight line. "This is very bad. Patty could have gotten hurt."

"We need to tell Officer Benson what we found," I said.

"Help! Security!" someone screamed.

Sonny groaned. "What now?"

Jennifer from the Sparkle Jewelry cart vaulted onto the stage. She ran up to Officer Benson. "Please help! My box of rings has been stolen!"

9

THE HEAT IS ON

Another theft! Ashley and I stared at each other. This case was getting totally out of control!

Officer Benson sprang into action. She shouted orders into her walkie-talkie. Then she turned to Jennifer. "I want you to show me exactly where the box of rings was," she said.

Jennifer led the way off the stage, her jewelry clanking.

"We need to talk to Officer Benson, too,"

Ashley told Tim. "Stay with Patty and wait for our mom, okay? She should be here any minute to pick us up. Tell her we'll be right back."

Tim nodded. Ashley and I climbed off the stage and hurried over to the Sparkle cart.

"The box was right here!" Jennifer told Officer Benson. She pointed to an empty spot on the cart.

"Did you see anyone suspicious?" Officer Benson asked.

Jennifer shook her head. Her dangly earrings bounced back and forth. "That thing on the stage fell and that girl started yelling. I turned around to see what was going on. When I turned back, the box was gone."

Officer Benson took notes on a little pad. Jennifer let out a moan. "There were fifty rings in that box!"

Ashley pulled me aside. "I'm taking

Jennifer off the suspect list, Mary-Kate. I don't think she would steal jewelry right off her own cart."

"You're right," I agreed. "Uh-oh. Officer Benson is leaving. We have to catch her."

"Officer Benson!" Ashley called. "Can we talk to you for a second?"

"Of course." Officer Benson turned around and headed over to us.

"I'm Mary-Kate Olsen. And this is my sister, Ashley. We're detectives. We've been trying to find a pin that was stolen from our friend Patty and—"

"There was another piece of jewelry stolen?" Officer Benson exclaimed. "You two really should have reported that!"

"We told Sonny Davis about it," Ashley answered. "He's the emcee for the talent show."

"He promised us he was going to tell mall security what happened," I added.

Officer Benson spoke into her walkie-talkie again. "Did anyone get a report of a pin being stolen from the talent show?" she asked. She raised the walkie-talkie to her ear and listened hard.

"It seems Sonny Davis never made the report," Office Benson told us. "I'll go talk to him."

"Great," Ashley said. "And we wanted to tell you something we noticed during our investigation. There were smears of chocolate on the cape Patty's pin was on. And there were smears of chocolate on the rope holding up the curtain."

"There was chocolate on the mouse cage, too!" I jumped in. "We think the thief let the mice out so people would get distracted. Then the thief could grab more jewelry."

"That's very interesting," Officer Benson said. She made a note in her little pad.

Tim trotted up to us. "Your mom is ready to leave now," he announced.

"You two had better go." Officer Benson smiled at us. "Thanks for all the great information. I'm going to go talk to Sonny Davis right this minute." She hurried away.

"That's funny. Why didn't Sonny report that the pin was stolen?" I asked.

Ashley tilted her head to one side. "Maybe he just got really busy with the talent show rehearsal," she answered.

"But maybe he never planned on reporting it," I said. "Maybe he's the thief!"

"I think he's our very best suspect," Ashley said as we made our way over to our mom and Patty. "Now we just need to prove it."

"What did you buy, Mom?" Ashley asked as we made our way out of the mall.

"A charm necklace for Lizzie." Mom held out a Sparkle Jewelry bag. "For her birthday."

I took the bag and looked inside. The

bracelet had animal charms on it. "Cute," I said.

"It's a surprise, so don't tell her," Mom continued. "Oh, and, Patty, I got a call from your mom on my cell phone. She returned home early from her trip."

"Oh, goody!" Patty said, smiling broadly. Then she pulled Ashley and me aside.

"Oh, *no*," she exclaimed. "My mother is home. She could find out I took the pin!" Patty hopped up and down. "If she does, she'll ask me where it is."

"Uh-oh." Ashley groaned. "That *is* terrible."

"I can't tell her it was stolen!" Patty's voice rose. "You guys *have* to find the pin." She grabbed our hands and squeezed hard. "You have to find it fast!"

X Marks the Spot

After dinner, Ashley and I changed into our pajamas. Then we went up to our attic office. Clue came with us. She lay under the desk and snored. That's how she does her best thinking.

Ashley sat in the desk chair. "We need to come up with a plan, Mary-Kate."

"Right," I agreed as I sat on top of the desk. "Tomorrow there will be a big crowd at the mall for the talent show. I bet the thief will be back. He or she will have lots of chances to steal more jewelry."

"And the mall police won't be able to watch everyone." Ashley pointed one finger in the air. "Only this time we'll catch him. I'm just not sure how."

"What if we trick him?" I suggested. "We can get the Sparkle Jewelry bag from Mom and put some of our fake jewelry in it. It's the perfect bait!"

Ashley clapped her hands. "Great idea. I'll walk around with the bag, and you watch me every second."

"When the thief snatches the bag, we'll catch him!" I cried.

"Super plan!" Ashley exclaimed. We grinned excitedly at each other. But slowly, my grin drooped.

"What if he's really sneaky?" I asked. "And we don't see him take the bag?"

Our plan needed to be perfect. Or we'd be left with no thief *and* no jewelry. And we would never find Patty's pin.

I jumped off the desk and jerked open the top drawer. "I've got an idea!" I rummaged through our detective supplies until I found our special pen. "Invisible ink. We'll mark the bag with some big X's. Then, when we shine a flashlight on our bag, the invisible marks will glow!"

"That should work," Ashley declared. "If we lose the thief, we'll be able to find him—"

"By finding our bag!" I said.

The next day, Patty and her mom came to pick us up for the big International Talent Show. We stopped by the Parks' house for Tim. Then we were off to the mall again. Now we would see who was smarter—Ashley and me, or the jewel thief.

Patty started biting her fingernails as her mom parked in the mall lot. I knew she was nervous. I couldn't tell if she was worried about performing without her lucky pin, or worried that her mom would find out the pin was missing. It was probably a little of both!

We stepped inside the mall and hurried to the stage. We passed a tall boy in a kilt tuning up his bagpipes and a girl wearing leather shorts softly practicing her yodeling.

"It looks like there will be some great acts in the show," Patty's mom commented.

Patty turned her face toward me. "I need my pin," she mouthed.

I nodded. "Ashley and I will be right back. Save us some good seats!"

"Hurry back, girls," Patty's mom called.

We jogged away from Patty, Tim, and Mrs. O'Leary. When we were out of their sight, Ashley took the Sparkle Jewelry bag out of her fanny pack. She stuck her wrist through the handle.

I looked around for the mall police. They were posted at every corner of the stage. Good. When I nabbed the thief, I wanted to make sure a guard was close by.

Ashley turned to me. "Ready?" she asked.

I gave her a thumbs-up. "Ready!"

Ashley strolled off. She held the bag so it was easy to see the Sparkle Jewelry logo. I followed close enough to keep her in sight.

As she passed the stage, I noticed Sonny testing the mikes. He glanced down at Ashley. Was he looking at her jewelry bag?

Ashley made her way past the Sparkle Jewelry cart. I hoped I would catch somebody watching her. But most of the people around were the moms and dads of kids in the talent show.

Next, Ashley walked past the Chocolates Galore cart. A line of customers waited to buy chocolate. Mr. Voler was busier than ever, but I saw him wave to Ashley.

"Ladies and gentlemen!" a booming voice announced. "Welcome to the International Talent Show!"

Colorful spotlights shone onstage. Sonny Davis jogged out from behind the curtain.

His hair was slicked back, and he wore a vest studded with silver sequins. "Welcome, parents, shoppers, and children from around the world," Sonny said. "We're about to get our show started!"

Ashley stopped. She leaned against a decorative planter to pretend to watch the show.

I hid behind two teenage boys and watched Ashley. She set the Sparkle Jewelry bag on the floor by her feet. Then she gave me a quick wink.

I shivered with excitement. I was sure the thief would grab that bag. And when he did, I'd be ready!

"For our first act," Sonny continued, "please welcome Michael Santino—the dancing Tower of Pisa!"

Michael climbed onstage, dressed as a huge tower. Opera music blared over the sound system. Michael threw his arms up and swayed left and right.

I glanced down at Ashley's bag. It was still there.

Next a girl wearing a kimono performed. Then the boy with the sombrero did his Mexican hat dance.

The jewelry bag stayed exactly where Ashley had put it.

After the hat dance, the crowd clapped wildly. Then Sonny returned to the stage.

"And now, Mr. Todd Le Bon will—"

"Ah-ah-chooo!" Mr. Voler let out another huge sneeze. The audience chuckled.

"Gesundheit!" Sonny called out. "And now, Ms. Sydney Johnson will yodel!"

I frowned. *That's weird. I thought Todd Le Bon was supposed to be the next act.*

Sonny quickly exited the stage as Sydney walked to the center of it. She cupped her palms around her mouth. Then she let out the loudest, longest sound I have ever heard. "Yodele-he-hooooooo!"

The last note was so high, I had to cover

my ears. It hurt them almost as much as the microphone screeching. And the sound seemed to go on forever!

When it finally ended, I turned my eyes to Ashley. She was cheering for Sydney along with the rest of the audience. I dropped my gaze to her feet and stifled a cry.

Oh, no! My mouth dropped open. I had taken my eyes off the bag for only a second! But now it was gone! The thief had struck again!

THE SNEEZE TELLS ALL

I raced over to my sister.

"Ashley! The bag!" I yelled over the cheering crowd.

Ashley looked down. When she noticed that the bag was missing, she looked as surprised as I felt. "I took my eyes off it for only a minute," she cried. "How could someone snatch it without me knowing?"

"It's not your fault," I assured her. "I didn't see the thief either. But he can't have gotten that far."

Ashley pulled out her flashlight. "Come on. We've got to find that bag!"

"Sparkle Jewelry bag on the left," I cried. "See the lady with the black jacket?"

"Got it!" Ashley rushed up behind the lady and aimed our flashlight at her bag. No X's. She wasn't our thief.

I turned in a circle. I scanned as much of the mall as I could see. "Oooh! Check out the guy with the beard by the Totally T-Shirts cart," I said. "He has a Sparkle Jewelry bag in his left hand."

Ashley raced toward him. I was only two steps behind her. She shined the flashlight on the man's bag. No X's.

"Who's next?" Ashley asked.

I checked the crowd, but I didn't see another Sparkle bag anywhere. "How did the thief get away so fast?" I asked.

Sonny's voice boomed out into the mall. "For our next act, please welcome Isabella Vega doing a classic flamenco dance!"

I turned and watched Sonny leave the stage. So did Ashley.

"Mary-Kate, are you thinking what I'm thinking?" Ashley asked. "Did Sonny have time to run off the stage and grab my bag?"

"Maybe," I said. "But we can't prove he did it. So now what?"

"Let's talk to Mr. Voler," Ashley suggested. "Maybe he saw someone run off with the bag! Plus, we never got to ask him about the people he's been selling chocolate to."

"The *millions* of people," I added.

We started walking toward the Chocolates Galore cart but stopped short. "Hey, look!" She pointed to the trash can on our right. A Sparkle Jewelry bag lay right on top.

Ashley flicked on her flashlight and pointed it at the bag. An X glowed yellowish green. "It's ours!" She gasped.

I picked it up. "It's empty. The thief took the jewelry and threw out the bag."

Ashley peered into the can. "No, he didn't."

She fished out the necklace and bracelet we had put in the bag.

My mouth fell open. "The thief threw away our jewelry?"

Ashley nodded.

"Why would he do that?" I asked. Then the answer hit me.

"Because he knew they were fake!" Ashley and I shouted at the same time.

Our thief was a real professional. No wonder he was so hard for us to catch.

"Let's hope Mr. Voler can give us a clue about who our thief is," Ashley said as we continued toward the cart. A lady in a white sweater stepped up to Mr. Voler just as we reached him.

"I want a box of chocolates," she said. "The red box, please. Red is my niece's favorite color."

"Nope, sorry. That one's not for sale," Mr. Voler answered. "But I'm sure your niece would love a different box."

"Everything she wears is red. Her room is almost all red." The woman reached for the red box. "Couldn't you just—"

Mr. Voler pushed the woman's hand away. "Sorry."

"That's weird," Ashley whispered. "Why won't he sell the red box to that lady?"

"That's not the only thing that's weird," I said. I pulled Ashley down behind the T-shirt cart. I wanted to keep watching Mr. Voler. But I didn't want him to spot us.

"He's dipping chocolates now. And he's not wearing any gloves. I thought he was allergic to chocolate!"

"You're right. He should be sneezing like crazy," Ashley answered.

"Remember how many times he sneezed yesterday?" I asked. "There was that really loud one right before the mike started screeching and Patty's pin was stolen."

"And another one right before the mouse stampede," Ashley said. She frowned. "That was when that necklace and bracelet were stolen."

My thoughts whirred around in my brain. There had been a loud sneeze right before two of the three thefts. Could the thefts and the sneezes be connected?

"Ashley, was there a sneeze before the curtain fell down?" I asked. "Before the tray of rings was stolen from the Sparkle Jewelry cart?"

Ashley's eyebrows scrunched together as she thought. "Yes, there was!" she exclaimed. "Jimmy had just come up to us. We were talking about all the breaks Mr. Voler gives him. Then we heard Mr. Voler sneeze!"

"All those sneezes have to mean something. Don't they?" I asked.

"I think so. Except…" Ashley hesitated.

"What?" I prodded.

"Except there is no way Mr. Voler could have stolen the jewelry. He was at his cart during all of the robberies. We saw him there!" Ashley pointed out.

"Right," I agreed. "But he's still touching chocolate without sneezing. And that makes him suspicious."

"I wish we could get a look inside that red box," Ashley said.

"We can," I told Ashley. "You get Mr. Voler's attention. I'll peek in the box."

Ashley straightened up and headed over to the cart. "Do you have chocolate-covered orange slices?" I heard Ashley ask.

"Sure do," Mr. Voler answered. "Milk chocolate. Dark chocolate. White chocolate. What's your pleasure?"

"That's the thing. My mom loves all three," Ashley said. "Can you dip each slice in a different chocolate?"

I made my move. I inched toward the far side of the cart. Mr. Voler's back was turned as he talked to Ashley. I dropped to my knees behind the cart so Mr. Voler couldn't see me.

"I'm pretty busy today," Mr. Voler told Ashley.

I raised my head just high enough to see the boxes of chocolate. Then I slid over a few inches so I was right next to the red one.

"If you could come back tomorrow, I'd be happy to do a special order for you," Mr. Voler continued.

I raised my head a little higher. I lifted the box lid. My gaze fell on the chocolates inside the box, cooling on wax paper. They were all lumpy blobs. As if Mr. Voler didn't care what they looked like.

Then my eyes widened. I stifled a gasp. One of the chocolates was shaped like a shamrock!

A SWEET END

I gave Ashley a thumbs-up. Then I got away from Mr. Voler as fast as I could. Ashley met me behind the T-shirt cart.

"You are not going to believe this," I burst out. "Ashley, I'm sure I saw Patty's pin covered in chocolate! I don't think Mr. Voler is dipping candy. I think he's dipping jewelry. Mr. Voler must be the thief!"

Ashley's mouth fell open. "What? But we just said that was not possible. Mr. Voler was working at the cart. He didn't have time to rush to the stage and steal the pin. His cart is too far away."

I snapped my fingers. "That means he must have an accomplice—someone working with him! I bet he's using those sneezes to signal his partner, who steals the jewelry while he's at the cart."

Ashley frowned. "Maybe. But who could his partner be? And why would Mr. Voler cover Patty's pin with chocolate?" Ashley asked.

"Good question." I crept up toward the edge of the T-shirt cart and peered at Mr. Voler. He was putting more chocolates into the red box.

"I bet that red box is filled with chocolate-covered jewelry," I whispered. "That's why Mr. Voler wouldn't sell the box to that lady."

"We will now have a short intermission," Sonny announced from the stage. Several people—including Sonny—headed for Mr. Voler's cart.

"Here's our chance," I whispered. "Mr.

Voler will be busy with all the customers. Let's grab the box and bring it to security."

Ashley nodded. We headed for the cart. We were almost to the red box when Mr. Voler picked it up—and sold it to Sonny!

Ashley and I rushed back to our hiding place behind the T-shirt cart. "Mary-Kate! If the red box has the jewelry in it, why would Mr. Voler sell it to Sonny?"

"Because Sonny is Mr. Voler's partner," I answered. "They're working together!"

"That's it!" Ashley cried. "Mary-Kate, you're a genius. Mr. Voler sneezes when he sees someone wearing or buying something expensive. Then Sonny causes a distraction—like the squealing microphone or the escaping mice—and steals the jewelry while no one is looking!"

"Later, Mr. Voler covers the jewels with chocolate," I guessed, "so Sonny can buy them and take them from the mall without anyone knowing."

"But what about our bag?" Ashley asked. "Sonny didn't cause a distraction when our bag was stolen."

"No, but he did announce Sydney's act instead of Todd's," I pointed out. "Sonny has been running rehearsals all week. He must have known how loud Sydney's yodel was. He switched the two acts after he heard Mr. Voler's sneeze."

"Come on," Ashley urged. "Let's find Officer Benson. She needs to catch Sonny with that red box."

"Hey, why are you guys hiding behind that cart?" Tim called out. He trotted over to us. "Patty's dancing next."

I saw Sonny glance our way. His face paled. He looked over at Mr. Voler, who frowned.

Oh, no. Our cover was blown! They knew we were watching them.

Sonny turned on his heel. He strode away from the cart—and away from the stage.

"He's going for the exit!" Ashley wailed.

"We can't let him get away. Somebody call security!" I yelled. I took off after Sonny.

"Wait, Mary-Kate!" Tim called after me.

I couldn't stop. I had to keep my eye on Sonny or we would lose the jewels forever. He pushed through the crowd. He picked up speed until he was almost running.

He was too fast for me. But I wasn't going to let him get away. I jerked off my backpack. I threw it at Sonny's legs—as if it were a bowling ball and he was a big pin.

The backpack knocked against the backs of Sonny's knees. He tripped.

The red box flew into the air. Chocolate-covered jewelry rained down on the mall floor.

I sprinted toward Sonny. I couldn't let him get those jewels back. I heard footsteps behind me and checked over my shoulder.

Tim raced toward me—leading the way

for Officer Benson and another guard. Before Sonny could climb to his feet, they had him handcuffed.

I picked up the empty red box and started scooping up the spilled chocolates. Tim ran over to help.

Ashley jogged up followed by two other guards. They were holding on to Mr. Voler. He was handcuffed, too.

"Hold on a minute, girls. If these guys are the thieves, where are the jewels?" Officer Benson asked us.

"Ow!" Tim hollered. "What kind of chocolates are these? It's like biting into a rock," he complained.

Ashley and I laughed. "That's because you're biting into gems. They *are* a kind of rock."

I turned to Officer Benson and handed her the red box. "The jewels are all in here. That's how they sneak them out of the mall," I explained. "Covered in chocolate."

Officer Benson took the chocolate from Tim. She scraped at it with her fingernail. Underneath was Patty's pin.

"Yes!" Ashley and I high-fived. Case closed.

"It wasn't until the end that we figured out the two thieves were using sneezes to signal each other," Ashley explained to Tim. The three of us made our way back toward the talent show.

"So Sonny was the one making all the distractions," I added. "He even let the mice out of their cages."

"I can't believe you solved the case!" Tim exclaimed. "You guys are the greatest detectives ever."

I blushed. "It's nothing, really."

"Ladies and gentlemen," a woman said into a microphone, "I'm Marsha, your announcer for the rest of this show. The next contestant will be Patty O'Leary."

We ran to the stage as Patty was about to make her entrance. "Patty!" Ashley whispered. She waved her hand in the air. I held up her pin.

Patty bounced up and down on her toes. "My lucky pin! Oh, thank you, thank you!" She wrinkled her nose. "Eeew. What's this brown stuff on the back of it?"

Ashley and I had picked the chocolate off the front, but we didn't have time to get it all. "Don't ask," I told Patty.

Ashley pinned the emerald-and-diamond shamrock to Patty's cloak.

Patty opened her mouth to say something more. But the music started and she ran up the steps to the stage.

I blew out my breath. "Just in time."

Patty started dancing, and we forgot all about the case. She stomped and kicked with her ghillies. Her shamrock pin shined in the light. But her smile was even brighter!

Hi from both of us,

Ashley and I were so excited for our school science fair. Our friends had the coolest projects, like an exploding volcano and a food pyramid made with real food. Our friend Jessie even made a walking talking robot!

But when Jessie's robot is stolen, the science fair is cancelled. It's up to us to find the robot and make sure that the fair goes on!

Want to find out more? Take a look at the next page for a sneak peek at our next mystery, *The New Adventures of Mary-Kate & Ashley: The Case of the Weird Science Mystery.*

See you next time!

The Case Of The
WEIRD SCIENCE MYSTERY

"Come on, guys," I told my sister, Ashley, and my friend Jessie. "We have to make it to Mr. Snyderbush's house before the teachers' conference ends."

Mr. Snyderbush was our science teacher. He loved building all kinds of gadgets. And we had a pretty good hunch that he knew where Jessie's missing robot was!

We walked up the stone path to Mr. Snyderbush's house. It looked pretty normal from the outside.

"Shh!" Ashley said. She put her finger to her lips. "Do you hear that?"

WHIRRRRR…WHIRRRRR!

I did hear it. And so did Jessie.

"Hey!" Jessie said excitedly. "That's the same noise my robot makes."

"Where is it coming from?" Ashley asked.

We followed the noise around the house to a cellar door.

"It's coming from in there," I said. I grabbed the handle on the door and pulled as hard as I could. The heavy door slowly creaked open.

Ashley peered inside. "It sure is dark in there," she said.

Jessie gulped. "Who knows what could be down those stairs," she said.

Ashley took a deep breath. "I'll go down first," she replied.

I watched as Ashley slowly walked down the concrete stairs.

Then I heard Ashley gasp. "Mary-Kate! Jessie! You'll never believe what's down here!"

The Ultimate Fan's Reading Checklist
mary-kateandashley
Don't miss a single one!

The New Adventures of MARY-KATE & ASHLEY

- ❏ The Case Of The Great Elephant Escape
- ❏ The Case Of The Summer Camp Caper
- ❏ The Case Of The Surfing Secret
- ❏ The Case Of The Green Ghost
- ❏ The Case Of The Big Scare Mountain Mystery
- ❏ The Case Of The Slam Dunk Mystery
- ❏ The Case Of The Rock Star's Secret
- ❏ The Case Of The Cheerleading Camp Mystery
- ❏ The Case Of The Flying Phantom
- ❏ The Case Of The Creepy Castle
- ❏ The Case Of The Golden Slipper
- ❏ The Case Of The Flapper 'Napper
- ❏ The Case Of The High Seas Secret
- ❏ The Case Of The Logical I Ranch
- ❏ The Case Of The Dog Camp Mystery
- ❏ The Case Of The Screaming Scarecrow
- ❏ The Case Of The Jingle Bell Jinx

Starring in

- ❏ Switching Goals
- ❏ Our Lips Are Sealed
- ❏ Winning London
- ❏ School Dance Party
- ❏ Holiday in the Sun

TWO of a kind

- ❏ It's a Twin Thing
- ❏ How to Flunk Your First Date
- ❏ The Sleepover Secret
- ❏ One Twin Too Many
- ❏ To Snoop or Not to Snoop?
- ❏ My Sister the Supermodel
- ❏ Two's a Crowd
- ❏ Let's Party!
- ❏ Calling All Boys
- ❏ Winner Take All
- ❏ P. S. Wish You Were Here
- ❏ The Cool Club
- ❏ War of the Wardrobes
- ❏ Bye-Bye Boyfriend
- ❏ It's Snow Problem
- ❏ Likes Me, Likes Me Not
- ❏ Shore Thing
- ❏ Two for the Road
- ❏ Surprise, Surprise

Super Specials:

- ❏ My Mary-Kate & Ashley Diary
- ❏ Our Story: The Official Biography
- ❏ Passport to Paris Scrapbook
- ❏ Be My Valentine

Available wherever books are sold, or call 1-800-331-3761 to order.

HarperEntertainment
An Imprint of HarperCollins*Publishers*
www.harpercollins.com

mary-kateandashley.com
America Online Keyword: mary-kateandashley

DUALSTAR
PUBLICATIONS

WIN a MARY-KATE and ASHLEY
Around the World Prize Pack!

Enter below for your chance to win great prizes including:

- A set of autographed books including *Our Lips are Sealed*, *Winning London*, *Holiday in the Sun* and *Passport to Paris Scrapbook*

- A video library including *Passport to Paris*, *Our Lips are Sealed*, *Winning London*, *Holiday in the Sun* and *You're Invited to Mary-Kate and Ashley's Vacation Parties*

- A *Mary-Kate and Ashley Travel in Style* doll giftset

You'll even get a personal phone call from Mary-Kate and Ashley!

THE NEW ADVENTURES OF MARY-KATE & ASHLEY™

Mary-Kate and Ashley Around the World Prize Pack Sweepstakes

OFFICIAL RULES:

1. No purchase necessary.

2. To enter complete the official entry form or hand print your name, address, age, and phone number along with the words "THE NEW ADVENTURES OF MARY-KATE & ASHLEY Around the World Prize Pack Sweepstakes" on a 3" x 5" card and mail to: THE NEW ADVENTURES OF MARY KATE & ASHLEY Around the World Prize Pack Sweepstakes, c/o HarperEntertainment, Attn: Children's Marketing Department, 10 East 53rd Street, New York, NY 10022, entries must be received **no later than July 31, 2002.** Enter as often as you wish, but each entry must be mailed separately. One.entry per envelope. Partially completed, illegible, or mechanically reproduced entries will not be accepted. Sponsors are not responsible for lost, late, mutilated, illegible, stolen, postage due, incomplete, or misdirected entries. All entries become the property of Dualstar Entertainment Group, Inc., and will not be returned.

3. Sweepstakes open to all legal residents of the United States, (excluding Colorado and Rhode Island), who are between the ages of five and fifteen on July 31, 2002, excluding employees and immediate family members of HarperCollins Publishers, Inc. ("HarperCollins"), Parachute Properties and Parachute Press, Inc., and their respective subsidiaries and affiliates, officers, directors, shareholders, employees, agents, attorneys, and other representatives (individually and collectively "Parachute"), Dualstar Entertainment Group, Inc., and its subsidiaries and affiliates, officers, directors, shareholders, employees, agents, attorneys, and other representatives (individually and collectively "Dualstar"), and their respective parent companies, affiliates, subsidiaries, advertising, promotion and fulfillment agencies, and the persons with whom each of the above are domiciled. Offer void where prohibited or restricted by law.

4. Odds of winning depend on the total number of entries received. Approximately 450,000 sweepstakes notices distributed. Prize will be awarded. Winner will be randomly drawn on or about August 15, 2002, by HarperCollins Publishers Inc., whose decisions are final. Potential winner will be notified by mail and will be required to sign and return an affidavit of eligibility and release of liability within 14 days of notification. Prize won by minor will be awarded to parent or legal guardian who must sign and return all required legal documents. By acceptance of the prize, winner consents to the use of his or her name, photograph, likeness, and personal information by HarperCollins, Parachute, Dualstar, and for publicity purposes without further compensation except where prohibited.

5. One (1) Grand Prize Winner wins a Mary-Kate and Ashley Around the World Prize Pack, consisting of the following: a set of autographed books including PASSPORT TO PARIS SCRAPBOOK, OUR LIPS ARE SEALED, WINNING LONDON, HOLIDAY IN THE SUN ; a set of videos including PASSPORT TO PARIS, OUR LIPS ARE SEALED, WINNING LONDON, HOLIDAY IN THE SUN, and YOU'RE INVITED TO MARY-KATE AND ASHLEY'S VACATION PARTIES; a MARY-KATE AND ASHLEY TRAVEL IN STYLE doll giftset; a Mary-Kate and Ashley sunblock; a 10 minute phone call from Mary-Kate and Ashley (subject to availability). Approximate retail value: $165.

6. Only one prize will be awarded per individual, family, or household. Prize is non-transferable and cannot be sold or redeemed for cash. No cash substitute is available. Any federal, state, or local taxes are the responsibility of the winner. Sponsor may substitute prize of equal or greater value, if necessary, due to availability.

7. Additional terms: By participating, entrants agree a) to the official rules and decisions of the judges, which will be final in all respects; and to waive any claim to ambiguity of the official rules and b) to release, discharge, and hold harmless HarperCollins, Parachute, Dualstar, and their affiliates, subsidiaries, and advertising and promotion agencies from and against any and all liability or damages associated with acceptance, use, or misuse of any prize received in this sweepstakes.

8. Any dispute arising from this Sweepstakes will be determined according to the laws of the State of New York, without reference to its conflict of law principles, and the entrants consent to the personal jurisdiction of the State and Federal courts located in New York County and agree that such courts have exclusive jurisdiction over all such disputes.

9. To obtain the name of the winner, please send your request and a self-addressed stamped envelope (excluding residents of Vermont and Washington) to THE NEW ADVENTURES OF MARY-KATE & ASHLEY Around The World Prize Pack Sweepstakes, c/o HarperEntertainment, Attn: Children's Marketing Department, 10 East 53rd Street, New York, NY 10022 by September 1, 2002. Sweepstakes Sponsor: HarperCollins Publishers, Inc.